P9-CEV-209

To everyone who feels like they don't fit in. Stay different. You're unique and special. —T. L.

To all those who know there's no such thing as NORMAL. —S. B.

STERLING CHILDREN'S BOOKS
New York

An Imprint of Sterling Publishing
1166 Avenue of the Americas
New York, NY 10036

STERLING CHILDREN'S BOOKS and the distinctive Sterling Children's Books logo
are trademarks of Sterling Publishing Co., Inc.

Text © 2016 by Tara Lazar
Illustrations © 2016 by Stephan Britt
The illustrations for this book were drawn and painted by hand, then assembled digitally.

All rights reserved. No part of this publication may be reproduced, stored in a retrieval system,
or transmitted in any form or by any means (including electronic, mechanical,
photocopying, recording, or otherwise) without prior written permission from the publisher.

ISBN 978-1-4549-1321-4

Distributed in Canada by Sterling Publishing
c/o Canadian Manda Group, 664 Annette Street
Toronto, Ontario, Canada M6S 2C8
Distributed in the United Kingdom by GMC Distribution Services
Castle Place, 166 High Street, Lewes, East Sussex, England BN7 1XU
Distributed in Australia by Capricorn Link (Australia) Pty. Ltd.
P.O. Box 704, Windsor, NSW 2756, Australia

For information about custom editions, special sales, and premium and corporate purchases,
please contact Sterling Special Sales at 800-805-5489 or specialsales@sterlingpublishing.com.

Art direction and design by Merideth Harte

Manufactured in China
Lot #:
2 4 6 8 10 9 7 5 3 1
12/15
www.sterlingpublishing.com

NORMAL NORMAN

by TARA LAZAR

illustrations by S.britt

STERLING CHILDREN'S BOOKS
New York

Hello and welcome to "Normal Norman."
This is my first time narrating a book.
I'm a bit nervous. I hope it goes well.
My assignment today is to clearly
define the word NORMAL.

Allow me to introduce Norman. He will help me demonstrate the word *normal*. You see, Norman is EXCEEDINGLY normal.

In fact, we selected Norman because our scientists found Norman to be the most average animal on earth. Regular. Ordinary. A common, everyday creature.

Let us examine him.

Wait a moment, Norman.
What is that you're eating?

That is NOT normal, Norman.

Here, please have this banana instead.
A banana is normal.

And then, normal animals peel fruit and eat it—*quietly*. Here, try an orange.

Norman, this is not part of our "normal" presentation. Umm, next page, please!

Stop, oh stop, you wicked brute! I must save the yellow and orange creatures!

Next, we will present Norman's home.

NORMAL JUNGLE

NORMAL TREE

NORMAL CAVE

NORMAL WATERHOLE

Thank you, Norman.
You may rest a moment.

Hold on, Norman.
Animals do not sleep in bunk beds.

Here is a pile of leaves and branches.
Please lie down. This is normal.

Ah yes, Mr. Scruffles. That is your father, correct?
Let's move on to the next exhibit, then: Norman's normal family.

NORMAL MOTHER

NORMAL FATHER

NORMAL SISTER

NORMAL BROTHER

NORMAL STUFFED ANTEATER

Normal stuffed anteater?!
Norman!

An animal with his own stuffed animal? This is ABNORMAL!
Please, let's take a five-minute break to straighten all this out.

Just a second, Norman.
Who are you talking to?

My best buddy.

Your *friend*? You cannot be friends.
You are natural enemies in the wild!
This is exceptionally strange.
Most. Certainly. Not. Normal!

Please, Norman, you are being very disruptive.

I'm getting outta here!

Norman, animals do not drive dune buggies!

Or fly with dual-rocket jet packs!

Or dive in deep-sea submersibles!

This is definitely, positively NOT NORMAL!

This is crazy. This is absurd! This is ruining my perfectly normal demonstration!

I have failed to show my readers what normal means. Everything has gone wrong. This is a disaster! I will never be asked to narrate a book again!

Ahem. Pardon that brief interruption. We were experiencing temporary technical difficulties. Let's return to our presentation.

We are about to see Norman's friends in their natural habitat. Please note how normal they are.

As you can see . . . umm . . .

. . . everyone likes being his or her normal self.

And so do I! Enough of this book narrating stuff. I quit!

I need to get back to my normal hobby.
Want to join me, Norman?